Inside this book:

23 story pages, 10 Foil Art pages, and
4 thin foil transfer sheets enclosed in a pocket inside the cover,
plus a sheet of silver stickers for you to decorate your pictures.

Use pencils and the stickers to complete the story pages.
You cannot use the thin foil transfer sheets on these pages.

The Foil Art pages are for you to decorate and embellish
with the foil transfer sheets. Please follow the steps below.

✦ Peel away any of the shaded shapes to reveal a sticky surface.

✦ Rub on a foil sheet of your choice, ensuring the foil's dull side
   is face down on the paper, with the bright side **facing up**.

✦ Gently peel away the foil to reveal your foiled picture.

If you need more foil to complete your Foil Art pictures,
thin foil transfer sheets can be
found at most craft stores.

Based on the story by
Gabrielle-Suzanne Barbot de Villeneuve

Once upon a time there lived a handsome prince. Despite having everything that he could ever want, he was greedy and cold-hearted. To teach the prince a lesson for being so unkind, a fairy cast an enchantment over him and his castle, turning him into a formidable beast, and his servants and attendants were frozen in time, leaving the Beast quite alone.

The fairy told the prince that there was only one way for the enchantment to be broken—he had to learn how to love and be loved in return. Should he not find love, the enchantment would not be lifted, and he would stay a beast forever. As the years slowly passed by, the lonely Beast became more and more convinced that no one could ever love such a grotesque creature.

Not far from the castle there lived a merchant and his six children—three sons and three daughters. Once a wealthy businessman, the merchant's family was now forced to live a simple life in a crumbling countryside cottage. While his three sons and two of his daughters were deeply unhappy, wishing for their former lives of luxury where they did not have to work, his youngest child, Beauty, loved the new life and cozy cottage. If she wasn't completing her chores, she would likely be found with her nose in a book, for that's what she loved to do most. Beauty was also very beautiful, with wealthy suitors often asking for her hand in marriage. But Beauty was kind-hearted and rejected all proposals in order to stay and care for her father. Her positive outlook and her love for their father led Beauty's sisters to be intensely resentful and bitter toward her.

One day, Beauty's father left on a journey to seek his lost fortune. He asked each of his children what they would like him to bring back. They asked for jewels and expensive clothes, all except for Beauty, who asked simply for a single rose. The father's journey was unsuccessful, and upon heading home empty-handed, he became lost as he traveled through a deep forest in a storm. As the storm began to die down, he stumbled into a moonlit clearing and discovered a gloomy castle among the trees. He decided to seek shelter at the castle, hoping he would find food and a warm place to sleep.

The castle door was open, and the halls led to a room with a table laden with food and a bed to sleep in. Not once did the man see a servant or his host. In the morning as he was about to leave, he discovered an exquisite garden. Remembering Beauty's request, he picked a single rose for her. The Beast appeared; he was furious that the merchant would steal from him and threatened to throw the man into the dungeons. After much pleading, the Beast eventually agreed to let the merchant return home to say goodbye to his family on the condition that the man returned to be his prisoner.

When the merchant returned home to tell his children of his agreement, there was an uproar. Beauty's sisters declared that it was all her fault. Beauty, however, calmly told her father that she would take his place instead. Despite her brothers' protests and her father's pleading not to go, she followed her father to the castle and begged the Beast to allow her to take her father's place as prisoner.

The Beast agreed, and Beauty was made the lady of the house. To her joy she was given free rein over the Beast's spectacular library.

For three long months, Beauty lived in the castle with the Beast. Despite loathing him at first, Beauty soon realized he was good-natured and kind, not the wild animal she had first assumed he would be. During the day she spent most of her time exploring, as well as reading the many books in the great library, and every night both Beauty and the Beast dined together.

While Beauty was happy, she missed her father terribly and longed to see him again. She begged the Beast to be allowed to visit her family. Seeing how much it meant to her, the Beast reluctantly agreed to let her go, but only for one week. As a gift he gave her a magic ring, which would bring her back to him, and an enchanted mirror so she could see him, if she wished.

The next day, Beauty returned home to her father. He was overjoyed to see his youngest child again and called for all the family to come home. Her sisters, now both unhappily married, were envious of Beauty's happiness and of her beautiful clothes and jewels. The spiteful pair decided to concoct a cunning plan to ruin Beauty's happiness, and they asked her to stay longer in the hope that it would anger the Beast so much that he would harm her when she returned. However, Beauty, overcome with gratitude that her sisters were finally showing kindness toward her, agreed to stay a little longer.

Despite being glad to be home and to once again care for her father, Beauty missed the Beast and thought of him often. On the tenth night, she suddenly remembered the enchanted mirror he had given her as a gift. Once she had found it, she looked into the mirror, wishing to see the Beast. Beauty gasped in horror as the mirror showed him lying among the roses of his garden, slowly dying. Beauty suddenly realized the terrible mistake she had made in leaving the Beast for her unloving, bitter sisters.

With one twist of the ring on her finger, Beauty was instantly transported back to the castle. She ran straight for the rose garden, where the mirror had shown the Beast. The Beast lay still amongst the flowers. Beauty fell to her knees in tears, confessing her love for him.

As her teardrops fell on the Beast's quiet body, Beauty was suddenly blinded by a dazzling ray of white light shining from the Beast. Within seconds more rays erupted, and before her eyes the Beast was transformed from an intimidating monster into a handsome prince.

Fireworks burst forth from the castle walls as the dark and dreary castle changed into a magnificent, dazzling palace. As if by magic, all the castle's servants appeared again—the butler, chambermaids, and footmen—all who had been trapped by the fairy's enchantment were finally free!

And Beauty and the prince lived happily ever after!

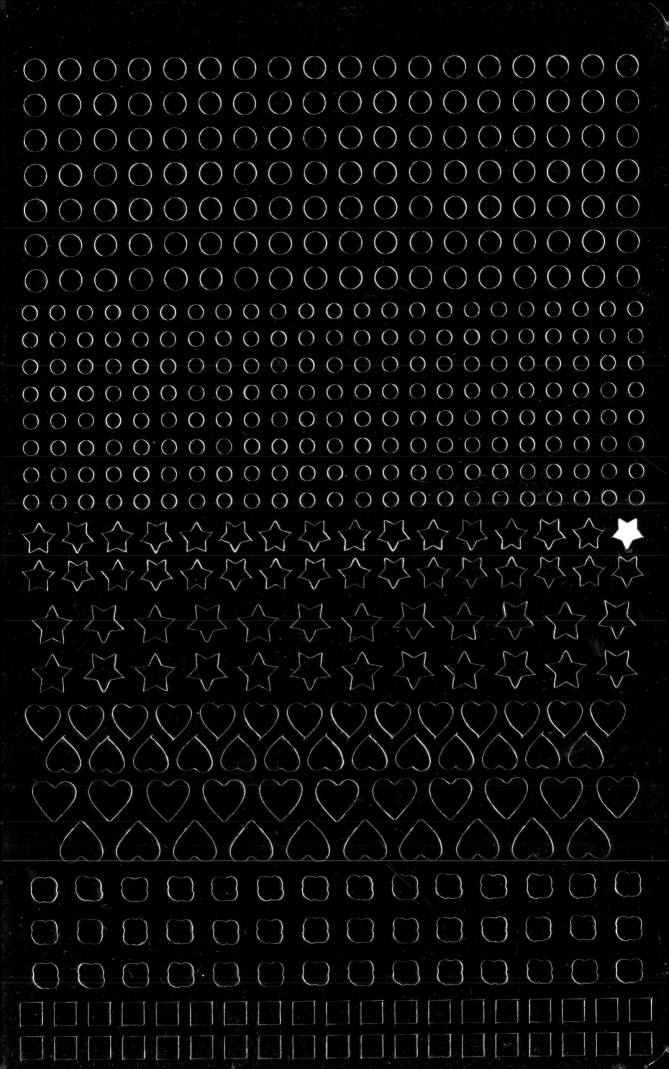